P9-CFS-756

Disney's Animal Stories

New York

TABLE OF CONTENTS

THE UGLY DUCKLING
Lost and Alone 1

BAMBI
The Prince Is Born 21

THREE ORPHAN KITTENS
The World Is a Wonderful Place 35

THE LION KING
The Circle Continues 49

THE JUNGLE BOOK
The Bear Necessities 65

CINDERELLA
If Mice Can Be Horses 87

101 DALMATIANS
Pups in Danger 107

BAMBI
The Winter Trail 127

TARZAN
The Best Ape Ever 137

THE FOX AND THE HOUND
Friends—No Matter What! 157

TABLE OF CONTENTS

A BUG'S LIFE
Every Ant Has His Day 171

POCAHONTAS
A Raccoon, A Dog, And a Bird—Oh, My! 187

THE LITTLE MERMAID
There's No Friend Like a Fish 205

THE RESCUERS
We Make a Great Team! 215

DUMBO
The Biggest Ears Ever 233

LADY AND THE TRAMP
A Midnight Stroll 247

OLIVER & COMPANY
A Little Lost Kitten 265

THE ARISTOCATS
The Best Place to Be 281

THE LION KING II: SIMBA'S PRIDE
The Circle Is Complete 297

Written by Sarah E. Heller

Designed by Alfred Giuliani

The edition containing *Bambi, A Life in the Woods* by Felix Salten is published by Simon & Schuster.
101 Dalmatians is based on the original book by Dodie Smith, published by Viking Press.
Tarzan® Owned by Edgar Rice Burroughs, Inc. and Used by Permission.

Characters from the Disney film suggested by the books by Margery Sharp, *The Rescuers* and *Miss Bianca*, published by Little, Brown and Company.
Story based on the Walt Disney motion picture, *Dumbo*, suggested by the story, *Dumbo, the flying elephant*, by Helen Aberson and Harold Perl. Copyright 1939 by Rollabook Publishing, Inc.

Printed in the United States of America.

First Edition

1 3 5 7 9 10 8 6 4 2

This book is set in 20-point Cochin.

Library of Congress Catalog Card Number: 99-64154

ISBN: 0-7868-3257-6

Walt Disney's

The Ugly Duckling

Lost and Alone

Peck, peck, peck, came a tiny sound. Mother Duck felt movement beneath her. Excitedly she stood up to watch perfect fuzzy yellow heads emerge from their eggs. At last they had come into the world!

"One, two, three, four," quacked Father Duck, but one egg had not hatched yet. It was the biggest egg, the one that had made Mother Duck so uncomfortable while she sat waiting.

Finally it started to crack open. The ducks watched expectantly. Father Duck was quacking proudly until he saw a white head appear. *White!* he thought. The large duckling looked like a strange clown with a piece of eggshell on his head.

The white duckling smiled happily at his new family, but his family did not smile back. Mother Duck was quite upset. She hid the little yellow ducklings beneath her wing. "Where did *this* come from?" Father Duck quacked angrily.

Mother Duck was certain this was no child of hers.

Leading her beautiful yellow ducklings to the pond, Mother Duck kept an uncertain eye on the ugly youngster waddling along behind her.

Still, the white duckling was excited! He didn't understand that Mother Duck didn't want him around.

The poor little duckling thought the world was perfect and grand as he climbed on his mother's back in the middle of the pond.

"Quack, quack, quack," said the yellow ducklings. Mother Duck smiled at them proudly.

"Honk! Honk!" said the white duckling. The others stared at him. Ducks do not make honking sounds, thought Mother Duck. She pushed the strange and ugly white duckling off her back and swam away with her four perfect yellow ducklings.

Sadly, the white duckling watched the others swimming away from him. What did I do wrong? he wondered. He was lonely. This great new world was not so grand anymore. He swam in circles by himself.

Climbing ashore, he stopped to look at his reflection in the water. I'm an ugly duckling, he discovered. My feathers are white and my neck is long. No wonder Mother Duck did not love me. The ugly duckling hung his head and wept.

He waddled through the marshes wondering what to do. "Chirp, chirp," called four friendly little marsh birds. The ugly duckling climbed into their nest and snuggled with them.

Then the mother marsh bird threw a

worm to her children. The ugly duckling caught it easily. When the mother marsh bird saw this, she pecked and squawked at the ugly duckling and chased him out of the nest. The ugly duckling was so frightened that he ran and ran. When he reached the

water, he swam without looking where he was going.

Bang! The ugly duckling hit something hard. Nervously he looked up and saw a duck. The duck was smiling. A friend! thought the duckling. He did not realize that the duck was made of wood. He happily swam around it and climbed onto its back.

With a great big bounce, he dove into the water. The wooden duck bobbed up and down. Its stiff bill hit the duckling on the head.

Thinking his new friend was angry, the little duckling swam away. He was so sad that he did not notice the graceful swan family swimming nearby.

"Honk! Honk! Honk!" called the little swans curiously.

The ugly duckling opened his eyes in surprise. These creatures look and sound just like me, he thought. Can it be true? He blinked his eyes and they were still there, honking for him to join them. Joyfully, the white duckling splashed in the pond.

The little swans swam and played with him. The duckling was having so much fun that he forgot about being ugly. He had friends!

Then the mother swan appeared. She was more beautiful than anything he had ever seen. He looked longingly

at her graceful neck and white feathered wings, which curved so softly on her back. But when the little swans swam to her, he remembered that he did not belong. No one wanted an ugly duckling.

Downhearted, he swam away. "Honk! Honk!" called his friends. They did not want him to leave. Even the mother swan came close and bent her neck, stroking him tenderly. She wrapped her lovely wings

around him in a warm embrace. "My little lost swan!" she honked joyfully.

I'm a swan! he wondered happily. Surrounding him with their friendly faces, the swans welcomed him into their family.

Walt Disney's

Bambi

The Prince Is Born

"Wake up, Friend Owl," called Thumper, a young rabbit. "The new prince is born!"

Quickly the word spread, and all of the forest animals raced to see the newborn fawn. They all cheered when he tried to stand up, but his legs were

still very wobbly. "He doesn't walk so good," said Thumper truthfully, but the fawn's mother didn't care. She was very proud of her little son. "Whatcha gonna call him?" asked the bunny.

"I think I'll call him Bambi," replied the doe.

Thumper nodded his approval. "Yup, I guess that'll do," he decided.

When it was time for Bambi to explore the forest, Thumper was happy to help his new friend.

They hopped through a hollow log and over a fallen tree. When Bambi fell down, Thumper helped him along. "Get up," he said. "You can do it." When Bambi tried to talk, Thumper encouraged him. "That's a bird,"

Thumper pointed out. "Say *bir-duh*." Bambi loved this big world, and he loved learning new things.

Thumper showed him a colorful butterfly, which the fawn followed into a field of flowers. "Butterfly?" he asked, but Thumper explained that they were flowers. He showed Bambi how to smell their beautiful fragrance.

The fawn copied his friend, but a little black nose met his own. A bashful skunk appeared from under the blossoms. "Flower!" exclaimed Bambi.

Thumper exploded with laughter. "That's not a flower," giggled the bunny. "He's a little . . ."

But the skunk interrupted. He was happy to be compared

with the sweet-smelling blooms. "That's all right." He smiled. "He can call me Flower if he wants to."

Bambi enjoyed playing with his new friends that spring. Then onc day Bambi's mother led him to the meadow. The water in the stream fascinated him. As he looked at his reflection, another face appeared beside his

own. It was a fawn named Faline.

Bambi was startled. He ran away to the grassy knoll where their mothers stood watching. Bambi tried to hide behind his mother's legs, but she nudged him forward. "Aren't you going to say hello?" she asked.

Bambi was shy. He ran back to the stream. Faline laughed gently, teasing him. "You!" he shouted, and chased her, too. It was fun running with Faline.

Soon Bambi saw great deer bounding through the grass. They were strong and fast. Bambi followed them. He liked prancing around, holding his head high as if he had antlers like the stags.

Then suddenly they stopped short! All the forest creatures became quiet. Bambi stared with the others as the great prince of the forest walked by. He was the strongest deer among them, and his antlers had many

branches. Even the stags bowed their heads with respect. But Bambi was curious. He stared in awe until the great prince turned to look proudly at the little fawn. Bambi was his son!

Soon spring turned to summer, and summer to fall. The leaves fell to the ground, and the wind blew them away. Bambi stayed warm against his mother in the thicket. Then one morning he awoke to find the world had changed.

"Mother, what's all this white stuff?" Bambi asked.

It was snow! It felt cold and wet, but Bambi didn't care. He was excited as he ran about trying to dodge the snow falling from branches. Thumper was outside playing, too. "Bambi!" he called. "Look what I can do!" Hopping toward the pond, he slid onto the ice. Bambi couldn't believe his eyes!

"It's all right," Thumper assured him. He thumped his foot. "See, the water's stiff."

Bambi soon joined his friend, but his hooves slipped and his legs sprawled out from under him. Thumper pushed and shoved to help him stand, but he fell again and again and again.

Next they went to find Flower. It wasn't easy to wake him up.

"Why are you sleeping?" asked Bambi curiously.

"All of us flowers sleep in

the winter," he giggled, and he closed his eyes again.

Then Bambi and Thumper disappeared into the winter wonderland. The friends could not wait to find out what new surprises life still had in store.

Walt Disney's

Three Orphan Kittens

The World Is a Wonderful Place

On a farm in the country, three little kittens were born in a cozy barn. The straw was warm and comfortable. Purring contentedly, they fell asleep with their paws wrapped around one another.

When they could move around enough, the kittens

discovered the farmhouse. They tiptoed playfully through the rooms. They pawed at blankets dangling from beds. They scurried after a cricket that escaped between cracks in the floor. Then the three little kittens climbed on the farmer's large boot. The big man wasn't happy and he shook them off.

"One cat is enough!" the farmer bellowed. He told

his son to take the kittens into town. They could find homes there, he thought grouchily.

It was cold and snowy outside. The farmer's son put

the kittens in a gunnysack so that they would stay warm. He put the sack in his truck and drove toward town.

The kittens thought the bumpy ride was fun. It was cozy and dark in the sack, and they wrestled and cuddled and soon fell asleep. In fact, they were so content that when the farmer's son drove over a big bump and the gunnysack flew out of the truck and into the snow, they weren't scared.

The kittens emerged from the sack into a winter wonderland. What a beautiful world, they thought. Not one of

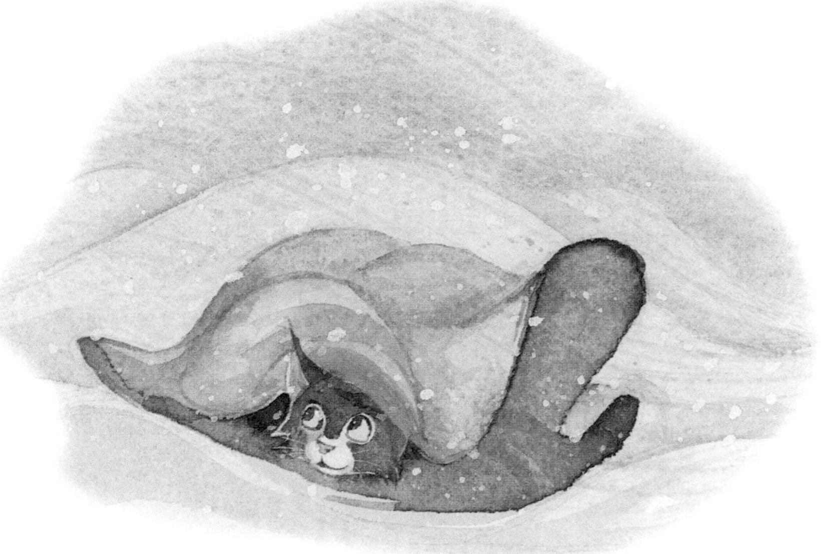

them realized that they were alone in the cold countryside.

Scampering into the deep wetness, the kittens batted the snowflakes and burrowed their noses in the snow. This is a fun place, thought the white kitten, sliding down a snowdrift.

But the black kitten wanted to explore some more. Curious, he pranced toward an open cellar window. The calico kitten and the white kitten followed their brother into the dark house.

Soon their little eyes were able to see

through the blackness. They noticed some steep stairs and began to climb toward a lighted doorway.

"Meow!" they called in their quiet voices, for the smell coming from upstairs was wonderful. As they finally pulled themselves to the door, they spied a

saucer of milk. Hungrily, they lapped it up, splattering their faces

and paws in their haste. Lick, lick, went their scratchy pink tongues, cleaning all of the milk from their fur.

It was warm in the room, and their tummies were full. Lifting their noses in the air, they followed a new smell coming from the tabletop. The three little kittens jumped up. It was a freshly baked pie! The crust felt warm on their paws, and the juice that squirted out was sticky but sweet as they licked it away.

They played on the table, but as the kittens moved about, the tablecloth buckled and slipped. Oh, no! The dishes and silverware and even the pie fell to the floor. Still, the kittens were not scared. The fall was delightful and the crash was a new and magnificent noise.

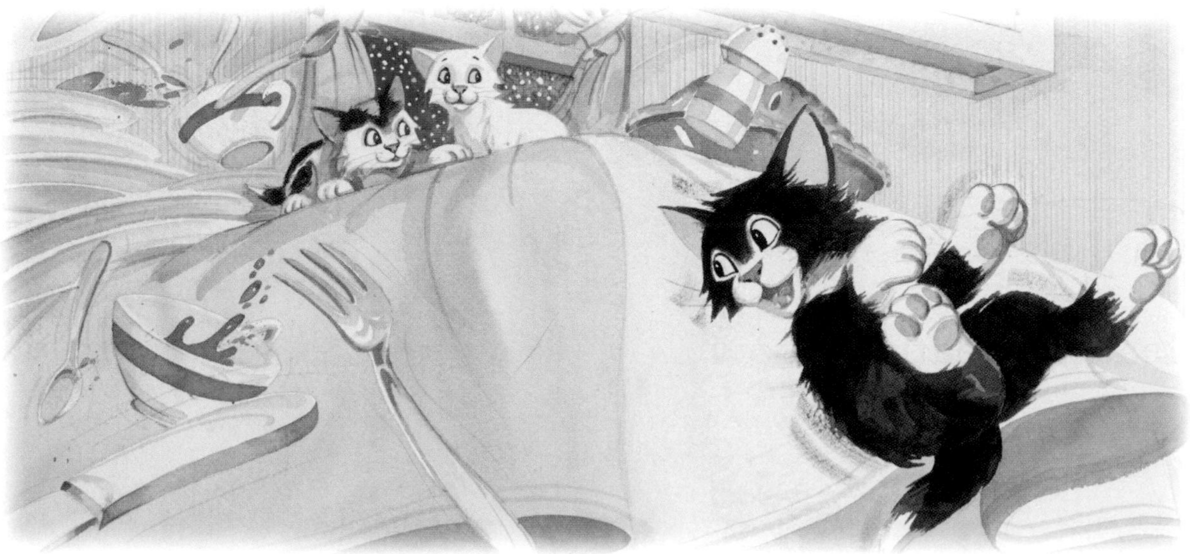

Scampering away, they found even more rooms in which to amuse themselves. Warm air coming from a grate in the floor kept the white kitten busy while his brothers pounced and meowed at a feather floating above.

Do, re, mi, fa, so, la, ti, went the piano as the kittens

discovered how to make delightful music beneath their paws. Stepping from key to key, they were startled when a large woman appeared. They ran as she chased them. Finally they escaped into a dark closet.

The closet belonged to a little girl. It was full of toys and shoes and fuzzy slippers. The kittens were exhausted from their busy day and curled up in a pair of sneakers and a soft pink slipper, and soon they were fast asleep.

"What sweet little angels!" whispered the young girl joyfully when she found them there. Scooping all three into a big hug, she knew she would love them forever. She named the sweet little balls of fur:

Fluffy, Muffy, and Tuffy. When the big woman saw the girl so happy, she grew to love the kittens, too.

As for the orphans themselves, they snuggled in the little girl's arms thinking that the world was a wonderful place indeed!

THE LION KING

THE CIRCLE CONTINUES

Mufasa and Sarabi were proud parents. The herds all bowed as Rafiki, the wise baboon, held their cub high, welcoming him to the Circle of Life.

"I was first in line to be king until that little *hairball* was born," Mufasa's brother, Scar, said scornfully as Simba grew into a playful cub.

Simba was unaware of his uncle's feelings toward him. One day, he even bragged to his uncle that he was going to rule the whole kingdom. Scar smiled slyly. He asked if Simba knew about the shadowy place.

"That's beyond our borders," Simba remembered.

Scar knew that an elephant graveyard, home to hyenas, would be the perfect trap for his unwanted nephew.

"Only the bravest lions go there," Scar told him. "And remember, it's our little secret."

Simba was excited. I'm brave, he thought. With his best friend, Nala, he conspired to lose their watchful guardian, Zazu, and make a journey to the forbidden land. "I just can't wait to be king!" Simba sang happily as they approached the elephant graveyard.

However, when hyenas began to chase the cubs, Simba realized that not all animals honored him as the future king. Simba tried to be brave like his father. He stood his ground and let out a roar. Suddenly Mufasa's

voice drowned out his own, and the great lion rescued the cubs.

Simba walked home in his father's footsteps, feeling very small. He knew he had made a big mistake and realized how much he still needed his father. "We'll always be together. Right?" he asked.

Mufasa looked toward the sky. "The great kings of the past look down on us from those stars," he told Simba. "They will always be there to guide you . . . and so will I."

Meanwhile, Scar was plotting with the hyenas. Still determined to make himself king, he made a

deal with the hungry animals. If the hyenas would help him kill Mufasa and Simba, Scar would give them the run of the Pride Lands.

Fortunately, Scar's plan was not completely successful. Although Mufasa was killed, Simba escaped from the hyenas by running through a forest of thorns. Hurt and exhausted, the young lion cub was rescued by a warthog named Pumbaa and a meerkat called Timon.

The two friends helped Simba forget his troubles in their jungle home. "Hakuna matata!" they sang. "It means no worries." Soon Simba adopted their carefree philosophy and put his past behind him. Learning to eat bugs, swim in the river, and play all day, the young cub grew into a strong lion.

One day Nala came to hunt in the jungle. When Simba heard Pumbaa call for

help, he charged the lioness. Quickly she flipped him on his back the way she had when they wrestled as cubs.

"Nala?" he asked in surprise.

"Simba!" she exclaimed. "You're alive! That means you're the king!"

As they walked in the moonlight, Simba felt confused. Seeing Nala again brought great joy but also painful

memories. Simba felt guilty for his father's death, and Nala could tell that he was troubled. They stopped to drink at a pond and gazed at each other thoughtfully. Not ready to answer difficult questions, Simba pulled the beautiful lioness playfully into the water and then chased her down the hill.

Still, he would not return to Pride Rock. Nala tried

to tell him that Scar and the hyenas had destroyed everything. "There's no food, no water. Simba, if *you* don't do something soon, everyone will starve."

In frustration, Simba ran away. I can't go back, he thought.

Then Simba heard a strange sound. Old Rafiki appeared. "Who are you?" Simba asked.

The wise baboon led him to a pool. "The

question is . . . who are *you*?" As Simba saw his reflection in the water, the lion saw how much he resembled Mufasa. "He lives in you!" cried Rafiki.

When the wind changed, Mufasa's image appeared among the stars. "Remember who you are," he told Simba. "You are my son and the one true king."

Understanding what he must do, Simba raced back to challenge his uncle.

"Step down, Scar!" he roared. The two battled while the lionesses overtook the hyenas. Using the trick that Nala had taught him, Simba flipped the evil lion over a cliff. Then, with a great roar, he reclaimed the land. Nala and the lionesses echoed his call. From that time on, Simba ruled the Pride Lands justly, respecting all creatures that returned to the kingdom. In turn, the

animals honored the Lion King and came to pay homage to his new daughter, Kiara. With Nala at his side, Simba watched proudly as Rafiki welcomed Kiara to the Circle of Life.

Walt Disney's

The Jungle Book

The Bear Necessities

Deep in the jungle, there was a mancub crying in the tall grasses. When Bagheera the panther found him, he brought the boy to a wolf den.

The mother wolf willingly took in the baby, Mowgli, and raised him with her cubs. However, when Shere Khan the tiger returned to their part of the jungle, Mowgli was not safe anymore. The wolves decided that he must return to the man-village.

Bagheera arrived to take Mowgli where he belonged. The boy climbed onto his back, ready for adventure. They ran all day. "Shouldn't we turn back now?" the boy asked sleepily, but Bagheera shook his head. "We're not going back this time," the panther told him.

Mowgli wanted to stay in the jungle. "I can take care of myself," he insisted.

Bagheera laughed. "You wouldn't last one day," he said as he pushed Mowgli up a tree to sleep.

Kaa the snake was watching them. While Bagheera dozed, Kaa looked into Mowgli's eyes, hypnotizing him. Then, as he wrapped his coils

around his young victim, Bagheera opened his eyes.

"Kaa!" roared Bagheera, and the loud noise roused Mowgli.

Kaa was not happy. "You just made a very big

mistake!" hissed the snake, but Mowgli pushed his coils off the branch before he could hurt Bagheera. *Thump! Thump! Thump!* The rest of Kaa's long body followed the coils to the ground.

The next morning Bagheera was ready to continue the journey, but Mowgli was stubborn. He held on to a

tree trunk and wouldn't let go. The panther tried to pull him, but Mowgli kicked with his feet until Bagheera fell into the water.

"I've had it!" cried the panther. "You're on your own."

Mowgli walked away. I don't need anyone, he thought as he sat in the shade.

Baloo the bear was dancing nearby but Mowgli didn't want company. He even punched the bear when

he came too close.

"Pitiful," said Baloo. Then he taught Mowgli to fight and

growl like a bear. The boy smiled at his new friend. "You're gonna make one swell bear," promised Baloo.

The mancub liked being a bear. They scratched their backs on trees and looked for food. Baloo sang as he tossed Mowgli a melon. Mowgli even floated down the river on Baloo's belly.

Suddenly, monkeys grabbed Mowgli! Laughing in the trees, they tossed him back and forth. Baloo tried to catch him, but the monkeys were fast. "Put me down!" yelled Mowgli, but they carried him away to their king.

Baloo didn't know what to do. "Help, Bagheera, HELP!" the stunned bear shouted.

At the ancient ruins, the orangutan, King Louie, wanted to make a deal with Mowgli. If Mowgli taught Louie how to make fire, then King Louie would keep

Mowgli in the jungle.

"But I don't know how to make fire," said the boy.

King Louie didn't believe him. He sang and danced around Mowgli, trying to convince the boy to confide in him.

When Bagheera

and Baloo arrived at the ruins they saw Mowgli dancing with the monkeys. Bagheera told Baloo to create a disturbance and then the panther would rescue the mancub. Baloo dressed up like a large female monkey. He danced with the monkeys and sidled up to King

Louie. But his disguise fell off. The monkeys weren't about to let Mowgli go without a fight. Soon, however, the ruins crashed down and Baloo had deposited Mowgli safely with Bagheera.

Later, as Mowgli lay sleeping, Bagheera convinced Baloo that the mancub wasn't safe in the jungle—especially

with Shere Khan waiting to pounce on him at any moment. Baloo knew that Bagheera was right, but he hated to see his young friend go.

The next morning Baloo and Mowgli were deep in the jungle heading toward the man-village. Mowgli wondered where they were going. Baloo gulped. "I need to take you to the man-village. It's where you belong," he tried to explain.

Mowgli was angry. "You said we were partners!" he yelled, running away.

Lost and alone, the boy encountered Kaa again. "You must trust me in order to stay in the jungle," hissed the snake, but Mowgli didn't trust anyone anymore.

He found a quiet place to sit and cry.

Shere Khan appeared! "I'm not afraid of you," Mowgli declared. He picked up a stick, prepared to

fight, but he didn't realize how fierce Shere Khan was. Suddenly the tiger lunged at him with sharp claws and teeth!

"No!" cried Baloo, running to his rescue. He grabbed Shere Khan's tail and stopped the big tiger in midair.

Lightning streaked across the sky, causing a fire nearby. Mowgli picked up a burning branch and tied it to Shere Khan's tail.

The mighty tiger ran for his life.

Baloo was lying still on the ground and Mowgli tried to wake him up. When Bagheera strode into the clearing, Mowgli looked to him for help. But Bagheera feared that Baloo was dead and he told Mowgli that he must be brave, like Baloo. "Oh, Baloo!" sobbed Mowgli.

"I'm all right, Little Britches!" called Baloo. "I was just taking five, you know, playing it cool."

The two embraced happily. Then Mowgli heard a strange voice singing. Climbing a tree for a better look, he saw a girl. She was beautiful. He had never seen

another mancub before.

Baloo and Bagheera watched him follow the girl. They could see that he was happy. "Let him go," urged Bagheera, and Baloo knew it was the right thing to do.

"But I still think he would have made a great bear!" he said.

Walt Disney's Cinderella

If Mice Can Be Horses . . .

"Wake up! Wake up!" sang the birds. But Cinderella was having a wonderful dream. She didn't want to wake up to another day of cooking, cleaning, and sewing. She flicked the little bluebird

gently with her finger, and he flew back to the window, chirping angrily.

"Serves you right, spoiling people's best dreams." Cinderella giggled. The birds and mice were her best friends. They always helped her get ready for her long days of work.

Suddenly Cinderella's favorite mouse friend, Jaq, came running for help. "A visitor! A visitor!" he cried. Quickly she followed the mouse. Indeed, there was a frightened mouse caught in a trap. "It's all right," Jaq told the mouse. "Cinderelly help you."

"We must give you a name," Cinderella told him after she had rescued him.

"How about Gus?" Gus nodded happily, and Cinderella made him some tiny clothes.

After Cinderella returned to her chores, the mice and their new friend, Gus, ventured downstairs for breakfast. "Lucifee's mean!" Jaq warned, pointing to

the cat, Lucifer. Then he skillfully distracted Lucifer as the other mice sneaked past. The mice grabbed some corn and ran back to the safety of their hole. Gus, however, had gathered too much corn and couldn't carry it all. Lucifer was waiting as the mouse scurried to pick up all his corn.

"Meow!" snapped Lucifer. Jaq watched in horror as his friend was chased. Thinking quickly, he pushed a broom onto Lucifer's head. Gus scurried up a tablecloth, but he wasn't out of danger. The mean cat soon had him trapped under a teacup.

Three bells were ringing as Cinderella hurried to get breakfast prepared. Putting teapots on the trays, she carried them upstairs, unaware that Gus was trembling under one of the cups.

"Mother! Mother!" screamed Anastasia moments later. "There's a mouse under my teacup!"

Lucky for Gus, Cinderella quickly figured out what had happened and raced to rescue Gus from under Lucifer's paw. Rushing to a mouse hole, Gus knew he owed his life to Cinderella.

When an invitation came to the King's ball, Gus decided that all of Cinderella's animal friends should help Cinderella. They knew she wanted to go to the ball, but there was no time to alter her dress. Her stepmother

kept Cinderella busy every minute.

The mice and the birds gathered needles and thread, singing as they worked. Gus and Jaq found some beads and ribbon that the stepsisters had discarded.

Happily, the birds draped them over a mannequin. The dress looked beautiful!

"Thank you so much!" cried Cinderella when she saw it. Dressing quickly, she ran downstairs, but her

stepsisters were jealous. "That's my sash!" said Drizella. "She's wearing my beads!" cried Anastasia, and they tore at the lovely gown until it was reduced to rags.

Poor Cinderella ran to the garden. As she sat down and cried, her friends watched her sadly. Suddenly the air sparkled and Cinderella's fairy godmother appeared! "Dry your tears," she said. "You can't go to the ball looking like that."

With a wave of her

magic wand, an ordinary pumpkin became a shining coach. Jaq and Gus couldn't believe their eyes when suddenly they were turned into horses. "Neigh!" whinnied Gus. He was excited to see Lucifer run away in fear.

"Now, don't forget," warned Cinderella's fairy godmother as the girl admired her sparkling new dress. "At the stroke of midnight, everything will be as it was before."

Cinderella heeded her warning, but as she danced with a handsome young man she forgot about the time. When the clock struck midnight she ran down the

steps, losing one glass slipper. "I'm sorry," she apologized to her animal friends after they escaped, "but he was so wonderful."

Cinderella's friends looked at her dreamily. She had fallen in love!

The next morning there was exciting news. It was about the Prince whom Cinderella had danced with at the ball. He had fallen in love with her and was trying to find her. At that very moment the Grand Duke was trying the glass slipper on every maiden in the kingdom.

"The Prince?" Cinderella was stunned.

When the stepmother realized that Cinderella was the mystery girl, she locked her in the attic. "Oh, no!" cried Cinderella. "You must let me out!"

Jaq and Gus were her only chance. Bravely they stole the key from the stepmother's pocket. Up, up, up the stairs they went, pushing and pulling the heavy key, until, panting and breathless, they reached the top.

Cinderella tried on the glass slipper and became the Prince's bride. As the happy couple ran down the stairs on their wedding day, the mice and birds cheered.

Disney's

101 DALMATIANS

Pups in Danger

In a town house in London, there lived a handsome couple named Pongo and Perdita who loved each other very much. Their human pets, Roger and Anita,

and the cheerful housekeeper, Nanny, lived with them. They were very happy, especially Perdita. She was expecting puppies!

One stormy night the puppies arrived. Roger

puffed his pipe nervously as Pongo paced back and forth. "Fifteen puppies!" announced Nanny from the other room. She came out to congratulate Pongo. "And the mother's doing fine, love."

Pongo was overcome with pride and happiness. As Roger danced him around the room, Anita smiled happily.

"Can you believe it, Rog? Fifteen puppies!"

Suddenly the door burst open! Uninvited, Cruella De Vil entered from the darkness. "Fifteen puppies!" she exclaimed

with an evil gleam in her eye. "How marvelous!"

Roger didn't like Cruella. When she wanted to buy the puppies, Roger got red in the face. "We're not selling the puppies!" he shouted. "Not a single one!"

Cruella glared angrily. "Keep the little beasts! But I warn you . . . I'll get even. You'll be sorry!"

Anita was proud of Roger for standing up to Cruella. Pongo was happy, too. He nuzzled Perdy gently as they lay with their puppies. "That devil

woman's gone," he told her. "The puppies are safe."

For a while, all was well. The puppies were playful and mischievous. Pongo and Perdy

loved them very much.

Then one night after the puppies went to bed, a couple of thugs named Horace and Jasper sneaked around. Cruella would pay them well for this job, they thought, as they found the sleeping puppies and took them to an old house in the country.

Pongo and Perdita were heartbroken! They listened desperately as Roger and Anita did everything they could to find the puppies. "Isn't there any hope?" Perdita asked Pongo.

The Dalmatians decided to take matters into their

own paws. They used the Twilight Bark to spread their plea for help quickly through the city and out to the country. Finally, a reply came! Puppies had been spotted at the old De Vil place.

"Oh, Pongo, it *was* her!" cried Perdita. They left immediately, running through the cold night. Finally, they found the broken-down mansion where Sergeant Tibs, a cat, was trying to keep the puppies away from Horace and Jasper. It was a hard job. Cruella had bought many puppies, and now there were ninety-nine.

Quickly Pongo and Perdita crashed through the window. Sergeant Tibs led the puppies away while the Dalmatians fought with the thugs.

"Cruella wanted to make dog-skin coats out of us!" exclaimed the puppies when Pongo and Perdita arrived, breathless.

They had to escape immediately. "We'll go to London," said Pongo.

They began their long journey home through snow and ice. The puppies grew tired and hungry, but luckily a collie offered shelter and milk in a dairy barn. Then a

Labrador assisted them in the town of Dinsford.

"I've got a ride home for you," said the Labrador, as the Dalmatians hurried into an old blacksmith's shop. Outside was a truck that would be leaving for London shortly. But Cruella had tracked them down! Furious, she

hollered to Horace and Jasper, "Get them, you idiots!"

The Dalmatians ducked low under the window as she peered inside. How would they ever get to the truck in time?

When Patch pushed Lucky into the fireplace, he was covered with black soot. It gave Pongo an idea.

"Let's all roll in the soot," Pongo told the puppies. "We'll be Labradors!"

At first his plan went well. In his disguise, Pongo led the puppies to the truck. Cruella watched suspiciously from her car as he loaded them into the back.

"Hurry, Perdy," called Pongo. "The van's about to leave."

As she emerged with the last group of puppies, it started to

rain. *Drip, drop,* splashed the raindrops, and the soot was washed away.

"After them!" cried Cruella.

Driving like a maniac, with her hair streaming behind her, Cruella tried to knock the delivery truck off the road. Horace and Jasper were racing toward the truck, too.

But the driver turned just in time.

Crash! Cruella's car collided with the thugs, and they went over the side of the hill.

Pongo and

Perdita sighed with relief. They couldn't wait to get home.

When they arrived with all the pups, Roger and Anita were overjoyed to see them.

"Oh, Pongo!" cried Roger.

"Perdy! My darling!" exclaimed Anita.

Nanny danced around the room, dusting soot off all the puppies as she counted them—one, two . . . ninety-eight, ninety-nine . . .

"A hundred and one Dalmatians!" she cried happily.

Pongo and Perdy were happy as Roger made plans to buy a country plantation where they could all live together.

Walt Disney's

Bambi

The Winter Trail

Bambi was warm and cozy in the thicket. When he heard a thumping sound outside, he yawned sleepily and stepped out in the cold snow.

"C'mon, Bambi!" called Thumper. "It's a perfect day for playing."

Shaking the sleep from his head, Bambi followed his friend. Indeed it was a beautiful day! The sky was blue and sunny, but the forest was still covered in a blanket of snow and shining ice.

"Look at these tracks!" said Thumper excitedly. "Who do you suppose they belong to?"

Bambi couldn't guess, so they decided to follow the trail. They pranced and hopped through the snow. It wasn't long before they came upon their first suspect, resting on a tree branch.

"Wake up, Friend Owl!" called Thumper. Friend Owl peered at the young animals in a huff. He had only just fallen asleep.

"Stop that racket!" he yelled.

Bambi and Thumper giggled. Owl was always grouchy when they disturbed his sleep. Deciding the footprints must belong to someone else, they continued on.

Soon they met up with Faline. She wanted to play, too.

"You can help us find out who made these tracks," said Bambi.

Thumper tried to wake up Flower, but hibernating was serious business. "See you next spring," he told them, with his eyes still closed.

As the friends walked on, they found a bird singing cheerfully. "Look! A red cardinal," said Faline.

"Maybe these are *his* footprints!" But the little bird chirped no, they were not *his* footprints.

A raccoon led them toward some woodpeckers. They were busy looking for food. "We didn't make those tracks," said the noisy birds. "We don't have time for walking around down there."

"Well, if these tracks don't belong to the woodpeckers, and they don't belong to the cardinal, and they don't belong to Friend Owl, whose can they be?" Bambi asked.

The three friends followed the trail to the end.

"A family of quails!" exclaimed Thumper.

The mother quail and her nine babies looked up from beneath the bramble bush. "Join us," Mrs. Quail cooed.

Bambi, Faline, and

Thumper were tempted to rest with the friendly birds. But suddenly the Great Prince of the forest appeared! He reminded them that the sun was setting. "Go home or your mothers will worry," he warned. Then, just as quickly as he had come, Bambi's father disappeared in the shadows of the tall trees.

"Look!" cried Bambi happily as all of their mothers entered the glen. Running under his mother's legs, the little deer stretched his nose up for a kiss.

"We've been looking for you," his mother told him tenderly.

Thumper was surprised. "How'd ya find us?" he asked.

Mrs. Rabbit pointed to his tracks in the snow. Laughing, the animals followed the trail back home.

Disney's

TARZAN®

The Best Ape Ever

Kala loved Tarzan as if he were her natural son. When he cried, she comforted him with songs and hugs. Tarzan loved his ape mother, and she was very proud of him. It didn't matter that he didn't look like everyone else. Kala knew that they felt the same on the inside.

Still, as Tarzan grew into a young boy, he was upset that

he wasn't as strong or as fast as his friends. He never stood a chance when Terk wrestled with him, and she was always leaving him behind when she went to play with her friends.

"Can I come?" Tarzan asked one day.

"Well, you could, if you could keep up," Terk answered.

She didn't expect Tarzan to follow her,

but he did. He was determined, and brave, too. When Terk dared him to get an elephant hair, he leaped off a cliff and swam into a herd of elephants.

"Piranha!" yelled Tantor. The young elephant had never seen anything that looked like Tarzan. Neither

had the other elephants. Frightened, they stampeded as Kerchak scooped up and saved a baby gorilla from being trampled.

Angrily, the great silverback Kerchak approached Tarzan. "You almost killed someone," he said. Kala tried to defend her son, but Kerchak wouldn't listen. "He will never learn to be one of us!" Kerchak growled. "Look at him!"

Tarzan was deeply hurt. He ran away and splashed angrily at his own reflection in the water. As he covered himself in mud to look more like the apes in his family, Kala watched him sadly.

"Why am I so different?" Tarzan asked her.

Kala tenderly placed Tarzan's hand on his chest, then on her own. She wanted to show him what she already knew. Inside, their heartbeats were the same.

"I just wish Kerchak could understand that."

Kala sighed.

"I'll be the best ape ever!" he declared as he hugged his mother.

True to his word, Tarzan grew into a young man with

amazing speed and strength. By imitating the animals around him, he learned many skills. Finally, he gained Kerchak's approval as he defeated a vicious enemy, Sabor the leopard.

Tarzan lay the dead leopard at Kerchak's feet, when suddenly a new sound alarmed them. Tarzan swung through the jungle toward the sound.

From a treetop, he looked down on the first humans he had ever seen. Never had another animal looked so much like him!

In their search for Tarzan, Terk and the others came across strange objects in the human camp. Tantor was terrified, but Terk calmed him.

"These things aren't *alive*!" Terk said.

As they investigated, they found that the typewriter made fun sounds. And the plates and silverware made music.

But their music brought others. And when Tarzan showed up with the humans,

Kerchak was furious. The humans ran off while Kerchak glared at Tarzan.

Upset and confused, Tarzan climbed a high

tree and spent the night alone. "Why didn't you tell me that there were creatures like me?" Tarzan asked Kala later.

She looked at him sadly. "Because it doesn't matter." She sighed. "You're my son."

Though Kerchak forbade him, Tarzan was drawn to the human camp. Every day he spent more and more time away from his gorilla family.

Brokenhearted, Kala finally brought Tarzan to the tree house where she had rescued him when he was an infant. "Whatever you decide, I just want you to be happy," she told him.

Instinctively, she knew what his choice would be, and her eyes

filled with tears as Tarzan hugged her.

"No matter where I go, you will always be my mother," he said sadly. Then, dressed in his human clothes, Tarzan was gone.

That night Kala couldn't sleep. As the other gorillas settled in their nests, she heard a disturbing sound. Just as Kerchak had feared, dangerous humans were closing in on them with nets and cages. Kala was terrified! Even Kerchak

was forced to the ground.

Then suddenly Tarzan appeared, freeing the ape leader.

As Clayton picked up his gun and took aim,

Tarzan snapped it out of his hand and smashed the gun on the ground. Clayton fled.

"You came," said Kerchak with surprise.

"This is my *home,*" Tarzan replied. He was determined to make things right. With help from Tantor, Terk, Jane, and other jungle friends, they soon had the hunters in the cages and the gorillas freed.

In the struggle, Kerchak had been shot and lay dying.

"Kerchak . . . forgive me," Tarzan said sadly.

"No . . . forgive me for not understanding that you have always been one of us," Kerchak replied, looking at Tarzan with respect and love. "Take care of our family . . . my son." Tarzan, knowing where he belonged, took his place as the gorilla leader and went to say good-bye to Jane.

Realizing that she'd never been happier than when she was in the jungle, Jane decided to stay. So did her father! The gorillas welcomed them warmly into their new family.

Disney's

The Fox and the Hound

Friends — No Matter What!

Tod and Copper were best friends. Splashing and swimming, neither the fox nor the hound had a care in the world.

"We'll always be friends, right, Copper?" asked Tod. Hugging each other, they promised to spend all of their days together.

However, Amos Slade had other plans for Copper. "You teach him to behave like a hunting dog," he told his old hound, Chief.

The next day, Tod wanted to play. He came looking for Copper. "Who's that big dog?" he asked his friend. Curiously, he walked up to Chief, who was sleeping in his barrel. Sniff, sniff went Chief's big nose. Even in his sleep he knew the scent of a fox.

"Grr . . . ruff!" barked Chief. Tod was scared. He ran fast. Amos came out with his rifle. *Bang! Bang!*

Poor Tod just barely escaped into the back of Mrs. Tweed's truck. "Get off my property!" Mrs. Tweed yelled at Amos. She had taken care of Tod since he was a cub and she was concerned about him. "Amos will not let

you get away next time," she said, cuddling the frightened fox. "You'll have to stay inside."

All through the winter, Tod waited for Copper. Big Mama, the owl, told him things would be different after

hunting season.

The night he returned, Tod crept quietly to see Copper.

"You have to go, Tod!" Copper warned. "I can't be your friend anymore."

Tod couldn't believe what he was hearing! Was it possible that Copper had forgotten all the great times they had spent together? Sadly, he turned to leave, but it was too late. Chief had woken up!

His loud barks woke Amos. "Get that fox!" yelled the hunter.

Copper couldn't let them kill Tod. Leading the hunters in the wrong direction, he tracked his friend. "Go that way," he told Tod, helping him escape.

The fox was happy. He knew

Copper still cared about him. But Chief did not. The big dog caught sight of Tod. He chased him to a bridge, but a train was coming! They were trapped.

Thinking quickly, Tod lay flat against the rails. The train passed over him. But Chief was too big. He had to jump.

It's my fault, thought Copper as he helped the injured dog. Chief was like a father to him. He felt guilty and angry, but most of all he blamed Tod. As Amos planned revenge, Copper joined him.

Meanwhile, Mrs. Tweed comforted her fox. She'd taken him to a wildlife sanctuary where he'd be safe.

"You'll be happy here," she sighed.

Poor Tod! He didn't understand, and the forest was a big and scary place. He felt lost and alone. But Big Mama was looking out for her friend.

She called another fox named Vixey to help Tod.

Tod had never seen anyone so beautiful! And when Big Mama appeared, Tod was overjoyed. Finally, everything would be okay.

Vixey and Tod spent the day together. She taught him how to fish. "Can I see you tomorrow?" he asked, and when Vixey nodded, he felt his heart leap.

Suddenly he heard a noise. *Snap* went a trap that Amos had set. Quickly, Tod and Vixey ran. Amos and Copper were right behind them. They crossed a great river on a fallen log. Panting breathlessly, Tod looked behind him. A bear had cornered the hunters.

Tod raced like he never had before. He was able to distract the bear. It followed Tod onto the log, but his weight caused the log to fall. Down a crashing waterfall went Tod and the bear. Weak and breathless, the fox collapsed on the shore.

"Now we've got him!" cried Amos. He pointed his rifle at the fox. But Copper stood in front of Tod. "If Amos shoots you, he'll have to shoot me, too," said the hound.

Amos nodded and walked away. Copper turned back to look at Tod. We'll always be friends, they both thought together, no matter what.

Disney · PIXAR

Every Ant Has His Day

On Ant Island, every ant knew his job. They followed one another in organized lines. It was a major catastrophe if a falling leaf divided them.

"I'm lost! I can't see the line!" panicked the ants.

It was Princess Atta's job to keep control. She was learning to take over the Queen's responsibilities and she was a nervous wreck. Would they have enough grain when the grasshoppers came to collect? she worried.

The Queen tried to calm her down. "Don't worry, dear," she soothed. "It's always the same: they come, they eat, they leave."

"Princess Atta, I've got to tell you something," said Flik, running into the anthill. His latest harvesting invention had knocked over the offering stone. All of

the grain had disappeared into the water.

"What have you done?" Princess Atta cried, but Flik didn't have time to answer. The grasshoppers had crashed through the walls of the anthill.

"Where's the food?" demanded Hopper.

Princess Atta was distressed as the bully pushed the

ants around and grabbed her sister, Dot.

"I want double the order of grain before the last leaf falls!" Hopper shouted. He didn't care that the ants would not have time to collect food for themselves before the rainy season.

As the grasshoppers flew noisily away, Flik had an idea. "We could get bigger bugs to fight the grasshoppers!" he exclaimed. Atta agreed to let Flik go search for bigger bugs. She didn't expect him to succeed, but this would keep him from causing any more trouble.

Floating away on a dandelion puff, Flik waved good-bye to Princess Dot.

"He'll get the bestest, roughest bugs ever!" the little princess told her Blueberry Scout friends.

When Flik returned with a group of the biggest bugs the ants had ever seen, Dot was excited.

"I knew you could do it!" she cried.

However, Atta was not so pleased. "We're ants. We don't fight grasshoppers," she said to Flik. She was suspicious of the warrior bugs. Could they really defeat Hopper and his grasshopper gang?

The large bugs were confused. "Flik! We're not warriors. We're circus performers!" cried Rosie the spider. There had been a misunderstanding. The circus bugs had thought that Flik was a talent scout. They wanted to leave.

Flik was devastated. "Don't go!" he pleaded, grabbing Slim the stick bug. If the other ants found out that he had messed up again, his life would be destroyed. "I'll come up with a plan. You won't have to fight. Just stay!" he begged.

They didn't have time to argue. A bird had swooped down and was about to eat Dot!

Francis the ladybug caught the tiny princess as she

fell and Flik gathered the other circus bugs to form a rescue party. Heimlich the caterpillar distracted the bird while Dim, a giant blue beetle, carried them all to safety in a thorny plant.

"Hooray!" cried the ants. Never had the circus bugs heard such applause! Blueberry Scouts wanted autographs. Even Atta was

congratulating the rescuers.

"We'll stay!" the praying mantis told Flik.

Soon the whole colony was working together on Flik's new design. They were building a bird to chase Hopper away and it actually worked. Flik laughed happily as he swooped down on the grasshoppers.

"Bird!" yelled Hopper. He was terrified as he looked at the ants that had squirted berry juice on themselves to look like they were bleeding. He and his grasshopper gang quickly ran for cover. But the bird caught on fire, and when Hopper realized that the ants had tricked him he was furious!

"Ants are losers!" shouted Hopper, but Flik

bravely stood up to the huge grasshopper.

"You're wrong!" he shouted. "You wouldn't be able to survive without us and you know it . . . don't you?"

The ant colony was mad. They knew what Flik said was true. But Hopper wasn't about to lose control. As he raised his foot to crush Flik, Atta stood in his way.

"This is the new order of things!" exclaimed the princess. "The ants pick the food. The ants keep the food. The grasshoppers leave!"

At that moment the entire colony charged! They overpowered the small grasshopper gang and were about to finish off Hopper when the rain started.

"Back to

the anthill!" shouted Atta. The weight and force of a raindrop could kill an ant. In the chaos, Hopper grabbed Flik and flew wildly through the storm.

"Flik!" cried Atta. She flew to his rescue, and they landed near a real bird's nest.

Thinking it was another trick, Hopper followed, but the mother bird grabbed him easily. Her babies were hungry.

Later, when the circus bugs left, they waved good-bye.

Disney's

Pocahontas

A Raccoon, a Dog, and a Bird—Oh, My!

Spoiled Percy sat on a pillow as Wiggins carried him to the ship. As the pet of Sir Ratcliffe, he was lazy and smug. Bones were his for the taking. His pillows were the finest and the fluffiest. Percy had an easy life as they sailed to the New World.

Meanwhile, across the ocean, an Indian princess was

playing with her forest friends. Meeko, a raccoon, and Flit, a hummingbird, were her constant

companions. Even when she dove from a high cliff, they followed her playfully into the river below.

"Your father's home," Nakoma told Pocahontas. Breathlessly, Meeko scrambled into the canoe and took

his usual lookout post. Flit hovered protectively as the Indian girls steered the canoe home.

When they arrived, Chief Powhatan was happy to see Pocahontas. He had good news.

"Kocoum has asked to seek your hand in marriage,"

he told her proudly. "He will make a good husband."

"But he's so serious," Pocahontas replied unhappily. Meeko agreed. He puffed up his chest and made a grim face, pretending to be Kocoum, but when Flit poked his belly he fell from the rafters into Pocahontas's arms. The silly raccoon could always make her laugh!

Still, Pocahontas was troubled. She

thought that the Dream-giver must want more for her than marriage to the unsmiling Kocoum. Grandmother Willow thought so too, as Pocahontas explained her dream about a spinning arrow.

"It is pointing you down your path," the wise tree spirit told her. "If you listen to the

spirits around you, they will guide you."

As Pocahontas wandered through the forest, Meeko and Flit followed. They were met with an unexpected sight; a large boat with sails that Pocahontas mistook for clouds. One of the white men was already ashore,

exploring the forest. They had never seen anyone like him.

Pocahontas was curious as she hid behind some bushes, but Meeko followed his stomach. He scurried toward the strange man and poked his nose in the stranger's bag.

"Is this what you're looking for?" asked John Smith.

He handed the raccoon a biscuit. Meeko nibbled happily.

Flit, on the other hand, was worried about Pocahontas. He poked at the newcomer, trying to make him leave.

But Pocahontas didn't want him to go away. Pocahontas felt that John had a good heart. As they got to know each other, she showed him how the land and water, the people and animals, were all connected to one another. They followed a bear and listened to the wolves. They ran among trees and meadows and swam with the otters. John Smith was fascinated with all that

Pocahontas had to teach.

Meeko was fascinated with John's bag. He was greedy for more biscuits but found a compass instead. It was too hard to bite, but he hoarded the new toy in Grandmother Willow's branches anyway.

Then the hungry raccoon followed John Smith to the settlers' camp. There was a lot of tension in the village. The settlers thought the Indians were dangerous savages and shot at any native they saw. Both villages were preparing for war.

Still, Meeko's mind was on food, and it wasn't long before he spied Percy's fine dinner. With a quick hand he shoved it all into his mouth. Percy was furious! Barking wildly, the dog chased the raccoon through

the forest.

However, their chase soon came to an abrupt halt. In a terrible struggle, John Smith had been taken prisoner and sentenced to death. Meeko, Percy, and Flit watched sadly as Pocahontas went to see him.

"No matter what happens, I'll always be with you. Forever," said John Smith.

Pocahontas was heartbroken. “What can I do?” she asked Grandmother Willow sadly.

Meeko wanted to help his friend. Trying to cheer her up, he handed Pocahontas the compass he had hidden.

There was the spinning arrow from Pocahontas’s dream!

Now the Indian

princess knew what path to follow. Running like the wind, she threw her body over John Smith, willing to give up her life to protect his. Pleading with her father, she made him see that hatred was not the answer.

Chief Powhatan laid down his weapon, but Ratcliffe had fired his gun.

"No!" yelled John. He jumped in front of the Indian chief, taking the bullet himself.

John would have to return to London to be healed, and Pocahontas was sad to see her friend go. But she was consoled to know that she was responsible for keeping the peace between the people.

Percy, Meeko, and Flit watched Pocahontas and John Smith sadly. Even *they* had learned to be friends.

Disney's The Little Mermaid

There's No Friend Like a Fish

"Don't be such a guppy," Ariel said to Flounder.

The small fish was afraid of the sunken ship. It was in a deep, dark part of the ocean. But Ariel was too excited to be afraid. Here was a chance to look for human treasures for her collection.

As the little mermaid put a pipe and a fork into her bag, Flounder's eyes grew large with terror. "A shark!" he yelled hysterically. Quickly, he

swam away from the razor-sharp teeth that were chopping right through the wooden boat.

"We're gonna die!" cried Flounder, but Ariel pushed him through a porthole. *Crash!* The shark was gaining on him! The shark followed the pair, but he was too big and got stuck in a hole.

"Take that, you big bully!" shouted Flounder as he followed Ariel to the surface. Whenever she found human

treasures she went to Scuttle the seagull to find out what they were.

"This is a dinglehopper," the silly bird said as he showed them how humans used it to comb their hair.

"I haven't seen this in years!" he exclaimed. Calling the pipe a snarfblatt, he blew into it hoping to make music. But all that came out was mud and seaweed.

"Music?" cried Ariel. "The concert! My father's gonna kill me!"

"The concert was today?" Flounder asked. He had forgotten all about it, and Ariel was supposed to be the star of the show. King Triton wasn't going to be happy.

As they arrived at the golden palace, the King and his trusted advisor, Sebastian the crab, were waiting angrily. "The entire celebration was ruined!" they yelled at Ariel.

Flounder tried to defend her. "It wasn't her fault," he declared. "A shark chased us.

Then a seagull came . . ."

"A seagull!" cried King Triton. "You went up to the surface again to see those barbarians?"

"But they're not barbarians," Ariel insisted.

"As long as you live under my ocean you will obey my rules!" he ordered.

Ariel was upset. She and Flounder swam away to their secret grotto without knowing that King Triton had sent Sebastian to keep an eye on them.

In shock, Sebastian listened to Ariel sing about her dream to be part of the human world. Her collection filled the grotto from floor to ceiling. Sebastian had never seen so many human things!

"What is all this?" he exclaimed. "If your father knew about this place . . ."

Ariel pleaded with him not to tell King Triton, but a

ship sailing overhead distracted her.

"Come back!" shouted Sebastian as she swam toward the surface.

The wind began to howl. It was a hurricane! The ship couldn't stand up to the might of the thundering waves and hot lightning. When it caught fire, men escaped to small boats, but still Sebastian and Flounder didn't see Ariel.

She was busy pulling a drowning human to shore. He

was so handsome. He was everything she had ever dreamed about!

Sebastian found her singing to the unconscious prince and didn't know what to do. King Triton would explode if he found out. "We're gonna forget this whole thing ever happened," he warned Ariel and Flounder.

Ariel swam around, singing to herself, dreaming of Prince Eric. More than ever, she wanted to become human.

"But down here's where

you belong," Sebastian said. She knew there was magic under the sea, but it wasn't what she dreamed about.

When Flounder came to show her a statue that had fallen in the shipwreck, she was delighted to see Eric's face in the stone. "It looks just like him!" she cried.

Flounder understood her dream to become human. He was the best friend a mermaid could have.

Disney's

The Rescuers

We Make a Great Team!

The Rescue Aid Society was gathered because someone had found a message in a bottle. It read:

To Morningside Orphanage

I am in terrible trouble.

Help, Penny

"Oh, the poor little girl!" cried Miss Bianca. She volunteered for the assignment and chose Bernard to

be her coagent. "We make a great team!" she said.

Bernard was stunned! He was just a janitor. But as he walked through the rain holding Miss Bianca's arm, he felt like the luckiest mouse in the world.

Soon they found Morningside Orphanage. As they scrambled

into a box of Penny's belongings, they heard a noise.

"Cat!" cried Bianca, but it was only Rufus. "I'm too old to be catching mice," he assured them.

Rufus loved Penny. He told them she was sad about not being adopted, but he didn't know where she was. "There *were* some nasty people from a pawnshop, who

tried to kidnap her once," he added.

Bernard

and Bianca thought they'd better check it out. At the pawnshop, the mice discovered a schoolbook of Penny's. She *had* been there!

Suddenly a phone rang, startling them. An ugly woman appeared and they ran for cover.

"Can't you control that little girl?" Medusa yelled into the phone.

"I'm taking the next flight to Devil's Bayou!"

Bernard and Bianca hurried to the airport. Dodging huge feet, they climbed aboard their albatross, Captain Orville. Bianca snuggled against Bernard as they flew into the sunset. What a lovely trip, thought Bernard, holding her close.

However, when they reached Devil's Bayou, there was an

explosion! Orville dodged fireworks and sped out of control, crashing in the marshes.

Soon Orville's swamp friends ran to help. They were glad to hear the mice had come to rescue Penny. No one wanted the little girl to be forced into that black hole again.

"You send Evinrude to get us if you need help," Ellie Mae told them.

Evinrude was a dragonfly. He had the fastest boat around, and the mice quickly climbed into his leaf as he steered them toward the riverboat where Penny was being kept.

"So you tried to run away?" they heard a man's voice scolding. "You better behave or I'll let the crocodiles have your teddy bear!"

Poor Penny! Bernard and Bianca hurried to help,

but the crocodiles chased the mice into an old pipe organ. *Do-re-mi-fa-so-la-ti!* sang the organ as Bernard and Bianca flew out of the pipes.

"We just have to rescue her," Bianca told Bernard.

When they climbed into her room, Penny was surprised. "Didn't you bring anyone big with you?" she asked.

The mice shook their heads. "But if we work together and have a little faith . . . " said Bianca.

"Things will turn out right," interrupted Penny. Rufus had taught her about faith, and her bottle *had* worked. Perhaps these mice *could* help.

Together they hatched a plan. Bianca was excited! But they would need help from the swamp folks. As Evinrude flew away, Bernard and Bianca hid in Penny's dress pocket.

"Oh, Penny!" called Medusa. "It's time to find the diamond!"

But Penny was afraid of the dark cave. "Please don't make me," she pleaded.

"Get down there, or you'll never see your precious teddy again!" yelled the evil woman as she grabbed Penny's bear.

The cave

was dark and spooky. There was a large skull with gaping eyes. “That’s where *I’d* hide a diamond,” said Bernard.

Sure enough, the diamond was hidden deep within the skull and they couldn’t get it out.

"It's stuck tight!" yelled Penny. "And the water's coming in!"

Still, Medusa would not pull Penny to safety.

"Use the sword," suggested Bianca.

It worked! Penny pried the skull open just in time.

Water filled the cave as Snoops hoisted them up.

"My diamond!" cried Medusa. She grabbed it and ran. Snoops and Penny followed. "Give me my teddy bear," cried the little girl, but Medusa had already hidden the diamond in its stuffing. She held Penny back with her rifle.

"Help!" cried the little girl, and the Rescuers put their plan into action.

With the help of their swamp friends, they trapped the crocodiles in an old elevator, tripped Medusa, and destroyed the houseboat with Snoops's fireworks. Grabbing her bear, Penny ran to the swamp boat.

The animals cheered joyfully as they made their escape and Bianca threw her arms around Bernard. "You were simply wonderful!" she cried, giving him a kiss. Bashfully, he smiled. They really did make a great team!

Walt Disney's

DUMBO

The Biggest Ears Ever

"Isn't he adorable?" cooed the lady elephants when they first saw the new baby. Mrs. Jumbo was beaming with pride! Lovingly, she caressed Jumbo Jr. with her trunk.

"Ah . . . ahh . . . CHOO!" The little elephant's sneeze shook his whole body and unraveled his large

ears. The lady elephants couldn't believe their eyes!

"How awful!" they cried, shaking

their heads disapprovingly.

"We'll have to call him *Dumbo*!" They laughed.

Mrs. Jumbo was furious! She went to the corner of the circus car and swept her baby toward her, cuddling him protectively. He was perfect in her eyes, and she loved him dearly.

Dumbo loved his mother, too. Playfully, he hid behind Mrs. Jumbo's legs, squealing with delight when she tapped him with her trunk. And when it was time for bed and his mother wrapped him up and rocked him to sleep, Dumbo felt safe and warm.

The next day they marched in the circus parade. People laughed when Dumbo tripped on his ears and fell in a mud puddle.

"Hey, look at the little elephant with the big ears!" shouted a boy. He and his friends teased Dumbo. They pulled his ears so hard that Dumbo fell down when they let go.

Trumpeting with rage, Mrs. Jumbo picked up a bale of hay and threw it to the ground.

"Mad elephant!" shouted the crowd, and Mrs. Jumbo was soon tied in chains and sent to solitary confinement. Poor little Dumbo was all alone.

Heartbroken, he sat in a corner and cried while the big elephants gossiped and snickered.

"It's all Dumbo's fault," they said, "with those ears only a mother could love." And when the little elephant walked toward them to eat some hay, they turned their backs on him.

Poor little guy, thought Timothy Q. Mouse. There he goes without a friend in the world.

Determined to do something about it, he followed Dumbo. "I'm your friend," he promised, offering a peanut. "I'll help you free your mother, but first we need to make you a star."

Although Timothy tried his best, Dumbo became a clown instead.

The other clowns painted his face and dressed him like a baby. Pretending to rescue him from a burning building, they threw water in his face. But most humiliating of all, they pushed him from the tall tower into a small bucket of water. Everyone laughed at the little elephant. Dumbo felt so ashamed!

After the show, he hung his head sadly as Timothy

washed away the paint. Big tears fell down his cheeks. Poor little guy, thought Timothy.

"Cheer up, Dumbo!" he said. "I'm taking you to see your mother."

The little elephant happily followed Timothy to the prison car. Mrs. Jumbo cried tears of joy as she rocked her baby, soothing him with a lullaby. And when they had to say good-bye, mother and son stretched their

trunks, holding each other as long as they could.

That night, Timothy and Dumbo had strange dreams. They were awakened by a flock of crows that were wondering how an elephant and a mouse had gotten so high in a tree.

When Dumbo opened his eyes and saw that his dream was true, he lost his balance. *Splash!* He and Timothy landed in a pond below.

"How did we get into that tree?" Timothy wondered. "Dumbo! You can fly!" he shouted joyfully, pointing to Dumbo's ears.

Giving Dumbo a feather, Timothy

encouraged him. "You can do it! Just flap your ears." Suddenly Dumbo was in the air. He was soaring!

Dumbo and Timothy were overjoyed!

They couldn't wait to show everyone at the circus. As Dumbo stood in the burning tower that night, he held the magic feather in his trunk. But when he

jumped, the feather slipped. He was falling fast!

"You don't need the feather!" cried Timothy. "You can fly without it!"

Seconds before hitting the ground, Dumbo spread his ears. Up, up he flew! He did loop-the-loops. He chased clowns. Dumbo even threw peanuts at the other elephants.

"You did it!" cried Timothy. Dumbo was a star!

Soon he was making headlines. People cheered wherever he flew. But best of all, Dumbo's mother was released from the prison car and they were together again!

Walt Disney's

Lady and the Tramp

A Midnight Stroll

Lady liked being a pet. Every day she woke Jim Dear for work. She brought him his slippers and fetched the newspaper. During the day, she kept

Darling company and they always enjoyed their walk together in the afternoon.

"Lady is getting so grown up," said Jim Dear one day. "I think it's time she had a new collar and license."

When he put it on her, Lady pranced happily outside. She was excited to show her best friends, Jock and Trusty.

"Aye, you're a full-grown lady now," Jock told her. Lady held her head high. She was so proud!

A few days later, on the other side of town, Tramp

was busy rescuing his friends from the dogcatcher. "Gruff!" he barked. As the dogcatcher ran after him, his friends escaped.

Tramp loved the chase! He tricked and teased the dogcatcher until he'd lost him. Then he looked around. "Snob Hill," Tramp muttered. "They've got a fence around every tree."

Curious, he wandered into a yard. There was Lady and her friends.

"Jim Dear and Darling have never acted this way before," Lady was saying sadly. But Jock and Trusty smiled. They knew what the problem was. "Darling's expecting a baby," Jock told her kindly.

Lady was confused. "What's a baby?" she asked.

"Oh, they're sweet and soft," said Trusty.

But Tramp interrupted. "When a baby moves in, the dog moves out!" he warned. Tramp didn't trust humans at all. He would never want to live behind a fence. "You'll see, Pidge," he told Lady. "It'll be leftover baby food for dinner and a leaky doghouse at night."

Lady was worried, but luckily Tramp's predictions did not come true. When the baby

was born, Jim Dear lifted Lady to the cradle. Darling pulled back the covers so she could see the tiny sleeping face. Lady loved the child instantly!

Every day she watched over the baby. She felt needed. Jim Dear and Darling petted her proudly. When they decided to take a short vacation, they knew the baby would be in good hands with Lady. Besides, Aunt Sarah would be there to help.

But Aunt Sarah did not let Lady near the baby. And

worse, she brought two sly and sneaky Siamese cats. They tried to eat the goldfish. They ripped the curtains. Then they smelled milk and began creeping upstairs.

The baby! thought

Lady. Panicking, she tried to stop the cats, but her barking angered Aunt Sarah. "We're going to get you a muzzle," she said, taking Lady to the pet store.

Lady was distraught! After the salesman put the muzzle on her, Lady ran out of the store. Cars screeched by her. Tin cans got caught on her leash and made a horrendous racket.

Ferocious dogs chased her. Lady was terrified as she ran into a dead end!

"Grr!" growled some large dogs. Then suddenly Tramp appeared! He attacked the bullies and rescued Lady. "Are you okay, Pidge?" he asked.

Sadly, Lady told her tale as Tramp listened sympathetically. "First, we've got to get this muzzle off," he said, leading her to the zoo. They found a beaver building a dam. With one bite, Lady was free.

Tramp wanted to cheer her up. He decided to take her to a special Italian restaurant. Tony, the chef, loved Tramp. He made spaghetti and even serenaded the dogs. As they ate a strand of spaghetti, their noses touched.

Generously, Tramp rolled the last meatball toward Lady.

It was a beautiful night. Lady and Tramp walked side by side through empty streets. The sky was lit with stars, and the moon was full. Lying on a grassy hill in the park, they fell asleep.

But the next morning Lady was worried. "I have to get home," she cried.

Tramp shook his head. "Come with me. I'll show you what a dog's life can *really* be," he told her. "Beyond those distant hills, who knows what adventures await us."

"But who'll look after the baby?" asked Lady. So Tramp took her back to her house.

Aunt Sarah was angry at Lady for running away. She chained Lady to the doghouse. Through her tears,

Lady watched a rat creep into the house.

Lady barked, trying to warn Aunt Sarah about the rat. But Aunt Sarah yelled at Lady to stop the noise.

Tramp heard her cries. "What's wrong, Pidge?" he asked.

"A rat! In the baby's room!" Lady barked.

Bravely, Tramp raced into the house. Lady broke from her chain and followed him up to the baby's room. Tramp fought the vicious creature.

But Aunt Sarah did not see the rat. She only

heard the crying baby. She locked Lady in the basement and shoved Tramp into a closet. She called the dog-catcher to take Tramp away.

When Jim Dear and Darling arrived home, they let Lady out of the basement.

"She's trying to tell us something," said Jim Dear.

Lady led Jim Dear upstairs and uncovered the dead rat. Tramp was a hero!

Gratefully, the humans thanked him. With a new collar and license Tramp soon became one of the leash-and-collar set. Still, he had no regrets. Soon, Lady and Tramp were smiling as four puppies and a baby played at their feet.

Walt Disney's

Oliver & Company

A Little Lost Kitten

On a sidewalk in New York City, five little kittens sat in a box. Many people walked by the box. Soon, all except one tiny kitten had been taken.

"Meow, meow," called the kitten. Rain filled the box with water, and the little kitten tumbled out, cold and wet. Still, the kitten looked at the people rushing past

him with hopeful eyes. But they were too busy, and the kitten was nearly trampled on the busy sidewalk. Scared and shaking, the poor kitten tried to stay out of the way.

Meanwhile, Dodger was roaming the streets looking for action. He was a street-wise dog. When he saw an opportunity, he took it. And the wet kitten was just what he was looking for.

"Relax, kid. I don't eat cats," said Dodger. "In fact, I'm looking for a partner to help me get some of the best sausages in town."

While the kitten distracted Louie, the hot dog vendor, Dodger grabbed a string of links and trotted away carefree. The furious kitten raced after him, over cars, through wet cement and building construction, to an old barge in the harbor where Dodger's friends were waiting.

"Half of those are mine!" yelled the little cat.

Dodger smiled at his spunk. So did the other dogs.

"We've never had a kitten in the gang before," said their human owner, Fagin. It was nice to feel welcome. Contentedly, the kitten tucked himself into the warm fur of Dodger's belly and dreamed about finding a child to love him.

The next morning, when the friends went in search of

money to help Fagin, they spied a limousine. This fancy car would do the trick, Dodger thought.

The kitten climbed into the limousine eager to help, but got lost in the giant car. When his friends gave up

and ran away, he was alone and afraid.

"It's okay, Kitty," said a gentle voice from the backseat. It was a little girl named Jenny. She reached over to untangle the kitten and cuddled him affectionately. The little kitten couldn't believe it! His dream was coming true.

In her house on Fifth Avenue, Jenny carried the kitten happily to the kitchen, where she made him a special meal. She named him Oliver and got him a special name tag. They played together at the piano and even took a walk in Central Park. Then, riding in a rowboat and a horse-drawn carriage, Oliver purred happily.

"I love you, Oliver," Jenny whispered that night as they lay in her warm bed.

Oliver purred contentedly. He rubbed his cheek against Jenny's, and they snuggled down to sleep. It had been a wonderful day . . . the best Oliver had ever had!

However, not everyone was happy with Jenny's new pet. There was a show poodle named Georgette who wanted Oliver out. So when Dodger and his friends

showed up the next day to rescue their friend, she happily threw the kitten into a bag for them.

Poor Oliver! Back at the boat he looked at the gang with sad eyes. "I wanted to stay with Jenny," he told them.

"But we rescued you," said Dodger, confused. His feelings were hurt. "You're a part of our family."

"I was happy there," Oliver told him. He didn't want Dodger to be upset, but Jenny was everything he'd ever dreamed about.

Just then Fagin returned. "Fifth Avenue!" he whistled excitedly when he saw Oliver's new license. *Dear very rich cat owner . . .* he wrote. He had come up with a plan to pay Sykes the money he owed.

It was dark and uncomfortable in Fagin's coat as they waited to collect the ransom.

Then he heard Jenny's voice. "I just want to get my

kitten back," she cried, "but I'm lost."

"*Your* kitten?" Fagin sighed.

He paced nervously back and forth, troubled. This little girl was innocent and sweet. "Don't cry," he told her. Guiltily, he handed Oliver to her.

"Oliver!" Jenny cried. The little kitten was overjoyed to be back in her arms!

Suddenly, headlights blinded them. In a flash, Sykes had grabbed Jenny, and Oliver had fallen out of her arms.

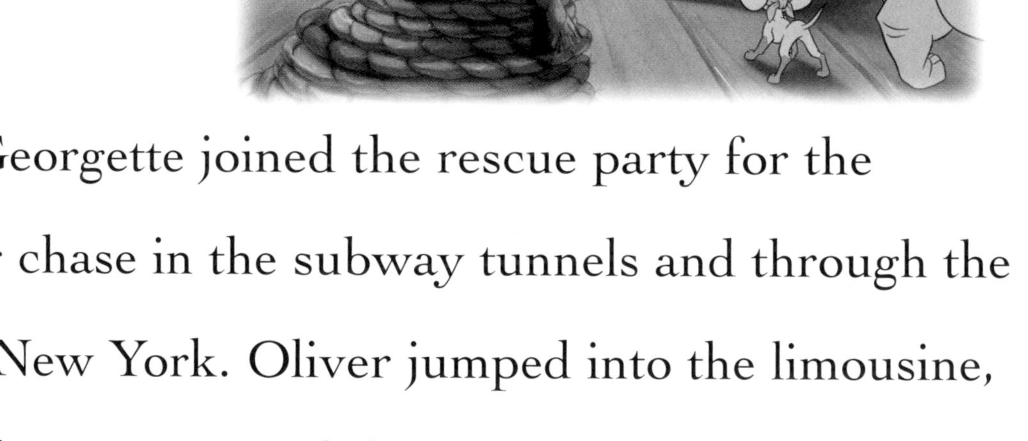

"Don't worry," Dodger promised Oliver. "We'll get her back."

Even Georgette joined the rescue party for the harrowing chase in the subway tunnels and through the streets of New York. Oliver jumped into the limousine, but Sykes's vicious guard dogs were ready to attack.

Racing through the streets and onto a bridge, Sykes chased Fagin with his limo.

The dogs got Jenny to safety as they raced onto a bridge that had been blocked off. Fagin swerved onto another track. Quickly, Dodger grabbed Oliver and jumped clear of the limousine before it collided with a train.

"Thank you," Jenny said to Dodger as they celebrated

together. She hugged Oliver tightly, and Dodger knew this was where the kitten belonged. Later, the gang joined Jenny for her birthday party and sang "Happy Birthday" to the little girl. As Jenny went to blow out her candles, she looked at Oliver lovingly. All of their wishes had already come true.

Walt Disney's

The Aristocats

The Best Place to Be . . .

In a grand house in Paris lived two fine ladies . . . Madame Bonfamille and Duchess. Of course, Duchess was a cat, but she was a lady nonetheless. She was even teaching her kittens, Berlioz, Toulouse, and

Marie, to be aristocats. Each day they had painting and music lessons. When the kittens teased one another, Duchess reminded them, "Ladies and

gentlemen do not fight."

They were all very happy with Madame. She loved them so much that she decided to leave her entire fortune to her pets.

Edgar, Madame's butler, was not happy; he wanted the money for himself. He plotted to get rid of the cherished pets. As Edgar warmed their cream that afternoon, he added

sleeping pills.

Soon Duchess and the kittens felt their eyes growing heavy. Climbing into their fancy bed, they fell fast asleep.

That night, Toulouse had a strange dream. He saw Edgar riding a motorcycle. They were bouncing in a basket. Dogs were barking. Then the basket was flying. . . .

But it wasn't a dream! The Aristocats woke up in the country, far from home. They were very frightened. As it started to rain, they huddled in their basket.

"Poor Madame," said Duchess. "She'll be so worried when she finds us gone."

Fortunately, the next morning was brighter. Duchess crept out of the basket to look around and was happy to see a friendly face. Strutting toward her was Mr. Thomas O'Malley, a charming alley cat.

Toulouse hissed like an alley cat, while Marie just sighed dreamily. She thought Mr. O'Malley was very handsome and romantic.

Laughing, O'Malley guided them all to a road and made a mark in the dirt. "This is where our magic carpet will stop," he promised. As he began to count, a milk truck drove around the bend.

"All aboard for Paris!" called O'Malley.

He even made breakfast magically appear. When the kittens closed their eyes, O'Malley uncovered a container

of milk. Marie, Toulouse, and Berlioz were impressed. They all thought O'Malley was the most wonderful cat in the world!

Then suddenly the truck came to a sharp halt! The angry driver had seen them and chased the cats away. "What a terrible man!" Duchess cried.

But O'Malley knew what to do. "Paris is this way,"

he told them, following the train tracks.

"Clickety-clack," sang the kittens, pretending to be a train. They made their way carefully across a bridge.

Then a loud sound frightened them all. A real train was coming!

Quickly, O'Malley pulled the kittens under the

tracks. They tried to hold on as the train rumbled overhead, but the shaking was too much for Marie. With a scream, she fell into the river below.

"Marie!" yelled Duchess. O'Malley dove into the water and pulled her to safety.

"Oh, thank you, Thomas!" cried Duchess gratefully. "What would we *ever* do without you?"

That night, they arrived in the city late. The kittens were tired, so O'Malley suggested that they sleep at his place. But as they walked toward the abandoned town house, they were surprised to hear music echoing through the walls. "It's Scat Cat, and his gang!" cried O'Malley happily.

Soon the cats were all swinging to the beat. "That's groovy!" called Scat Cat as Duchess danced with O'Malley. The kittens had never had so much fun!

"Stay with me?" O'Malley asked Duchess that night. They were sitting on the rooftop looking at the moon. It was very romantic.

She wished they could be together forever.

"But I can't," she decided reluctantly. "Madame needs us. I have to go to her."

The next morning, Duchess and the kittens went home. Edgar was not happy to see them. Desperately, he stuffed the cats into a trunk before Madame could find them.

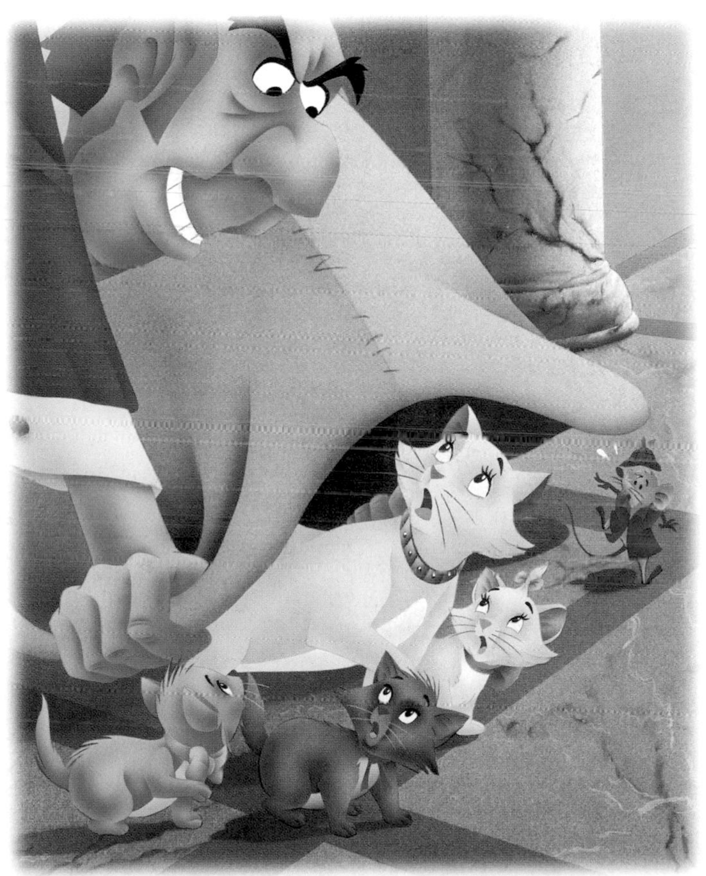

"This time I will get rid of you for good," he said, and he called a postman to come and take the trunk to Timbuktu.

But O'Malley arrived just in time to save his friends.

"Hiss!" he screeched, attacking Edgar. Soon the alley cats joined the fight. Even Madame's horse gave the butler a well-deserved kick in the pants, while Roquefort, the cats' mouse friend, unlocked Duchess and the kittens. Then they pushed Edgar into the trunk, just as the postman arrived.

"Oh, my darlings!" cried Madame as she took their picture.

It was truly a day to celebrate!

Madame adopted O'Malley, and he became part of the family. O'Malley was thrilled. He loved both Duchess and the kittens. In all his days as an alley cat, O'Malley never thought he'd settle down in a fancy pad like this! Yet in the whole world, there was no place he'd rather be.

THE LION KING II
SIMBA'S ◆ PRIDE

The Circle Is Complete

Simba paced nervously back and forth. He couldn't help worrying about his daughter, Kiara. Today was her first hunt, and there were so many dangers!

When Kiara emerged from the den, Nala caressed her proudly. Even Timon and Pumbaa cried tears of joy.

"Now, Daddy," warned Kiara, "don't interfere. Promise that you'll let me do this on my own."

Simba promised reluctantly, but as Kiara left, he secretly sent Timon and Pumbaa after her. The Outsiders were watching, waiting for a chance to avenge Scar. He couldn't take any chances with his daughter!

In the plains, Kiara was frustrated. The animals always seemed to hear her coming. How would she ever prove that she could be independent if this hunt wasn't successful?

Determined, she chased a herd of antelope over the hill. Pumbaa and Timon tried to get out of the way but Kiara saw them. She was furious!

"My father sent you, didn't he!" Kiara cried. Feeling betrayed, the lioness ran away.

But Simba had been right to worry. Zira, leader of the Outsiders, was setting a trap for Kiara. As they lit

the plains on fire around her, she collapsed, exhausted, in the grass. Then a lion appeared, lifting

the princess on his back to save her from the flames.

When Kiara opened her eyes, she was alone with the strange lion. He seemed familiar to her and she eyed him suspiciously. "Kovu?" she asked.

It *was* him! They had had so much fun as cubs . . .

until their parents had separated them. Pride Landers were not allowed to play with Outsiders. But now Kovu had saved her life. He should be allowed to return to Pride Rock.

But Simba still didn't trust Zira's son. For now,

Kovu would have to sleep outside of the cave.

From a distance Zira gloated. She had taught her son to hate. As soon as he was alone with Simba, Kovu would kill his enemy.

However, Kiara unknowingly interrupted the evil plan. Excited to spend time with her childhood friend, she persuaded Kovu to give her stalking lessons.

"Did you hear me coming?" she asked, after he evaded her pounce.

"Only a lot," he replied. Trying to show her how it was done, he jumped up a hill and surprised Timon and Pumbaa. The silly pair was trying to chase away a flock of birds.

"They're eating all the best bugs," moaned Pumbaa.

"Care to lend a voice?" Timon asked the lions.

With a roar, Kiara gave chase. Kovu followed easily, but he was confused. "Why are we doing this?" he asked.

Kiara laughed. "For fun!" she exclaimed.

Kovu had never done anything just for fun before. Running wildly, he roared with Kiara. It felt great until a rhino stampede chased them in the opposite direction. Ducking into a small cave, Kovu laughed with Kiara.

He had never had such a good time in all his life!

That evening, they lay in the grass looking at stars. Kovu felt very close to Kiara, but he was torn by his loyalty to his mother. What should he do?

Old Rafiki the baboon knew. Leading the lions to a

romantic place he called Upendi, he showed them what was in their own hearts. Kovu and Kiara had fallen in love!

Even Simba recognized the change in Kovu. That

night he let him sleep in the cave.

"I want to talk to you," Simba told Kovu the next day. As they went for a walk, the Lion King told Kovu the truth about Scar. Kovu couldn't believe how wrong he'd been! Determined to set things right, Kovu looked with admiration at Simba.

Then suddenly, Zira and her followers appeared.

"No!" cried Kovu, but he was knocked unconscious and the lionesses chased Simba. Desperately, he climbed a hill of loose logs and barely escaped the ambush.

The animals of the Pride Lands blamed Kovu. He tried to explain, but only Kiara believed him and when he was exiled, she followed him secretly.

Kovu couldn't believe she cared so much! Embracing her tenderly, they looked into the water.

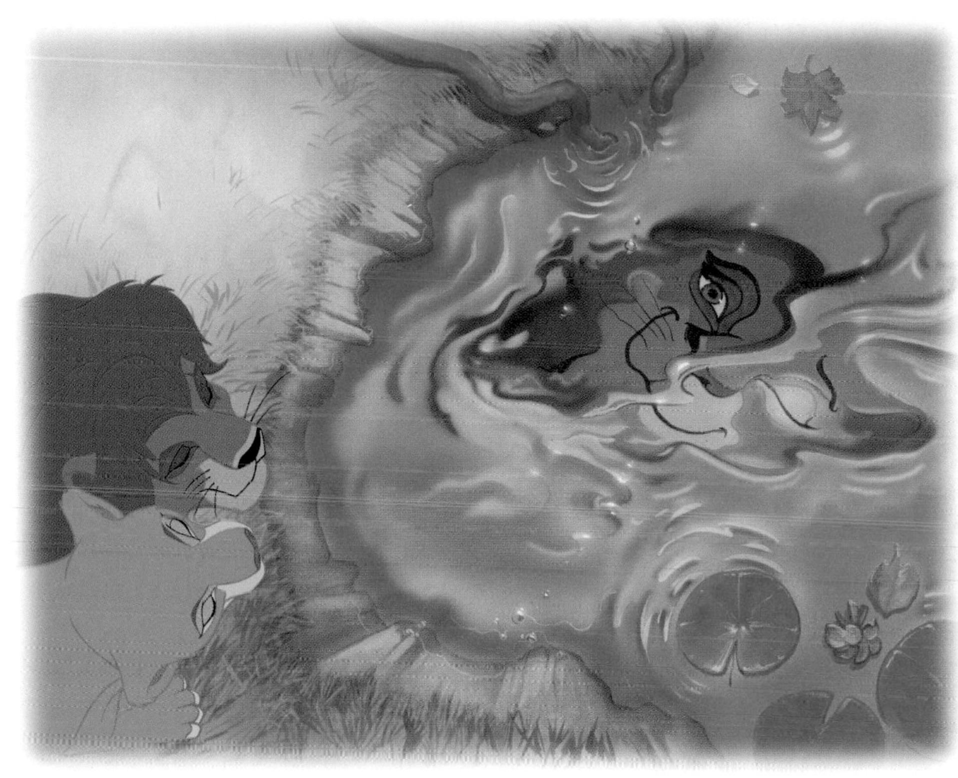

Their reflections merged as one.

"We have to go back," said Kiara quietly. "We have to stop the fighting."

Kovu knew she was right. They returned to find the battle about to begin.

"Stop!" cried Kiara. "Don't you see that we are one pride? We should stand together, not apart."

Simba looked at Kovu and his daughter. He could see their love. Even Zira's followers chose peace over fighting. But Zira would not give up! In a struggle, she fell into the raging river.

With her, the hate was swept away and a new peace

settled over Pride Rock. Nala and Simba warmly welcomed the new lionesses into the Pride, and they all rejoiced as Rafiki blessed the union of Kiara and Kovu.